DUMB

DUMBEST

THE DUMMY

Written And Illustrated
By
BRYHIMA .M . JOHNSON

First Published In 2016
By
Johnson Press Publishers
17 Daimler Way
Wallington
Surrey
SM6 8QX
ENGLAND.

Email: bryhima@btinternet.com

Mr Smart was a very polite boy, who never missed a chance to say please or thank you.

He was also known as THE DUMMY!!! because he always came
last in his year group.

All IN THE SAME CLASS.

THE ANIMALS AND MR SMART WHERE All IN THE SAME CLASS.
Mr COW WAS DUMB!
Mr GOAT WAS DUMBER!!
AND Mr SMART WAS THE DUMBEST!!!

To show how dumb he was he thought people were made from paper.

And animals where of vegetables.

Even Mr Goat stopped bickering and arguing with stupid people like him.

Well just imagine how stupid Mr Goat was to stop arguing with
Mr Smart, Oh dear.

Besides that he was also a very, very lonely boy because he was the only child in his family.

His parents got him a Dog call Brownie who was more clever than him.

The more he played with his dog, the more he forgot about
all the emptiness in his life.

And soon everybody got to like Brownie the dog.

"Isn't it wonderful to meet new people everyday on your walks with Brownie?" asked his Mum.
Mr Smart replied "yes it is Mother."

"Splendid I am so proud of you!!" said his Mum.
"Thanks Mum" he replied.

"I wish i had a brother!!" said Mr Smart.
"I am hoping to have a foster son will that be good enough?"
said his Mum.

"That's brilliant Mum, It will be wonderful to have a brother who loves dogs"
"I 'm not sure about that, but I promise he is a good boy"
"friendly people are always nicer to pets, Or have one themselves."

Well although Mr smart was a really, really, dumb person, He was a well mannered boy.

But all this was put to strain when his foster brother arrived.

He began to get wayward and missed deadlines.

He went partying and often stayed up all night.

Mr Smart's foster brother was a mouse who sat on social networking sites without studying.

Mr smart was disheartened as his hopes of getting better where fading away.

But as they say, your friends defined your personality.

So Mr smart stopped hanging out with dumb friends and chose to spend more time with his dog because he was the cleverest dog ever.

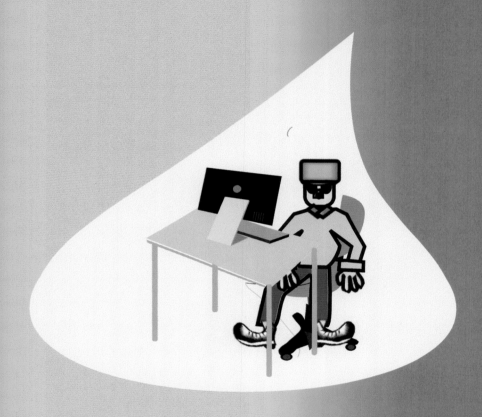

And failure was no longer a vow.
He stopped leaving school work till the last minute and met deadlines.

Ignoring problems where no longer an option.
bad behaviours where a thing of the past.

Soon he was counting from one to ten.

He also made a giant leap in reading the alphabet.

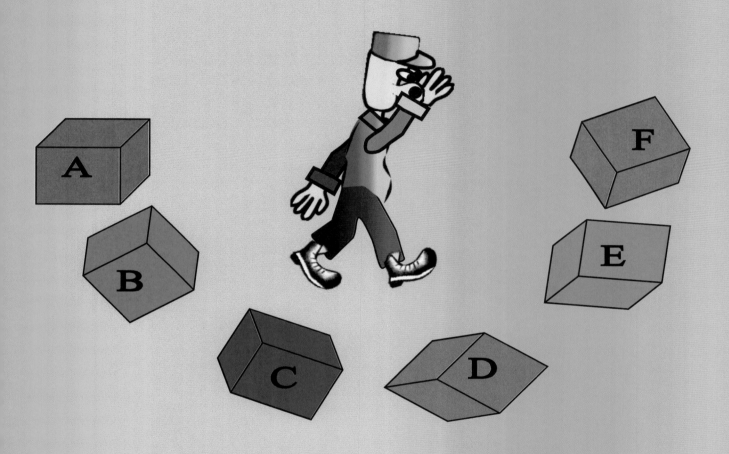

He proudly displayed his new skills to stupid Mr Goat.
"come on Mr goat, you can't afford my skills" said Mr smart.

Now watch, lets play guess a colour.

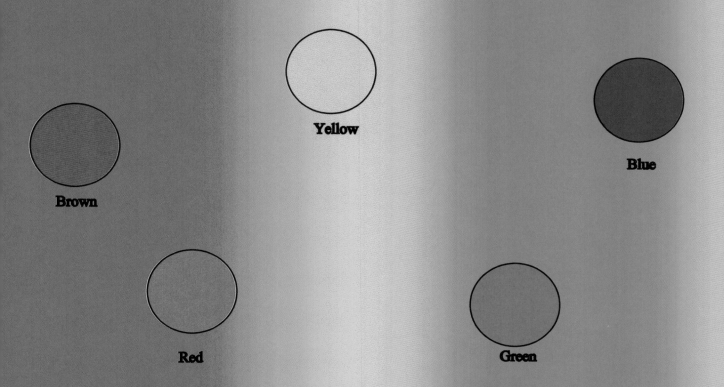

Yellow

Blue

Brown

Red

Green